STILL THE ONE

PRECIOUS JAMES

"STILL THE ONE"

Unless otherwise indicated, Scripture quotations are from the New Living translation and the New King James Version of the Holy Bible.

ISBN: 9798846221802

DEDICATION

To Jesus, my inspiration
Thank you.

CONTENTS

EPISODE 1

Still the One

We loved biology because it exposes us to some things about ourselves

•••

Our next topic is reproduction, kindly read up before the next class, our teacher announced as she left the class, we quickly swap through to the next chapter in our comprehensive and modern biology textbook to the long-anticipated topic, this class will be fun, and we trust our biology teacher she is so detailed, funny and vibrant, she will do full justice to this topic.

How time flies, Stephan and Stephanie the biracial (half-cast) twins were now in SS3 with their best friend Annabel Michael the commissioner's only daughter.

Stephen Donald was the senior prefect boy and Annabel was the senior prefect girl but she performs better at the chapel, she is slender with natural endowed features, she has a stunning eye like an ocean, her lashes are long and think, with a sharp cute nose, her smile runs over her eyes radiantly revealing her white array set of dentition dazzling, with dimples on both sides of checks. her fair skin glows, it is soft and spotless, she walks elegantly and gracefully, and she has this motherly vibe towards the students and problem-solving attributes to younger ones, Annabel and the twins have been so attached that they call themselves besties.

But lately, something unusual seems to be happening to Stephan

Ever since he overheard his classmates tripping for Annabel, how beautiful, caring, humble, and super intelligent she was, he taught to himself my bestie? He knows she was extremely pretty and intelligent but has never seen her in this new light.

Now he couldn't understand how he feels whenever he is around Annabel anymore.

As they work side by side in handling the school projects, butterflies kept on crawling in his stomach, he now noticed the way she smiles, her dimples, the way she talks when she answers questions intelligently, everything about her now caught his fancy, even the way she handles matters maturely, she is truly beautiful in and out he thought.

It was Tuesday during a break, Annabel was on the swing reading a novel, and Stephan walked up to her and sat close

They started discussing how boring the previous class was

Stephan: The class was pretty boring

Annabel: true. I almost dozed off she said smiling, I think the boredom came from his style of teaching

Stephan: Our next class is biology, topic, reproduction it will be so much fun, my guys have already penned down hilarious and weird questions to ask, and I can't wait, he said smiling

Annabel smiling said, naughty guys

As they both laughed, a leaf flew and stuck on Annabel's hair, wait!!! Stephan stretched out his hand to remove the dirt from her face

But suddenly stopped and started staring widely at her.

Annabel too became lost as she was staring back at him.

She raised her hand to remove the dirt and Stephan held it, she was beginning to melt, she thought she was stronger than that and just immediately the bell rang. And they left for classes

EPISODE 2

Still the One

I told you all to prepare for this topic and I guess you all have read through it.

The whole class echoed "yes ma'am" with excitement and jubilation

I am glad you all have read through it, it's a simple and easy-to-understand topic, so without wasting time we move to the next topic "Evolution"

Dismay and disappointment were written all over the student's faces as they reluctantly took lectures for the next class...

Annabel became uncomfortable around Stephan afterward, seeing Stephan makes her stomach growl and her heart race, what's wrong with me she asked, Am I in love with Stephan? No, it can't be, he is my best friend.

Now at her lonely times, she sees herself daydreaming before falling asleep, she would picture herself with Stephan like in all those Korean movies she loves watching, she would reflect on funny moments with him, and she would be smiling all to herself.

For some days she distances herself from Stephan, Stephan noticed at some point and felt bad, he was everyone's dream, a perfect description of a handsome boy, he is tall, with cute amber eyes and pink lips, like his Italian Dad.

Stephan and Stephanie’s mum, Avery Donald is from Nigeria but went for college at Italy where she met Grey Donald and they got married over the years, so the twins were born and brought up in

Italy, The Donald's parents decided to reside in Nigeria years later, so her mother and some of her family can keep watch on her children while she and her husband keep touring round the world and taking care of their business.

Mrs. Avery Donald was looking for the best school to enroll her kids in Nigeria, she was finding it difficult to choose a specific one, there were lots of suggestions from family and friends, making it overwhelming for her to make a decision.

She wanted only the best for her kids, they have been outside the country all through their lives, coming back she wants a school that will replicate what they had in Italy, she knew is almost impossible to find such in Nigeria, but she hopes to see something close. This time she wants them to go to a boarding school, so she can have time to herself, to tour around the world, and for their multi- international businesses scattered abroad. They have the luxury, wealth and comfort to give the twins the best of life.

It was during one her search she bumped into Kelly Michael, Annabel's mum

Kelly was her high school friend, and the two got along when they realized they were of a similar social class and financial status.

As she shared her frustrations with Mrs. Michael, Mrs. Michael recommended the school her precious daughter attends. Eden Noblex High School is a school for only billionaire kids she added.

All through her search, she has not come across this school, Eden High School accepts students only on referral grounds.

As Avery Donald arrived at the school, she was wowed, it was another world entirely, the school was like exactly of foreign school, It's a foreign school with an extension in Nigeria, all curriculum and activities are replicated in there also, this is what she has been looking for, their school fees was really high, could build an apartment but she was glad she would have peace of mind about the safety and wellbeing/welfare of her Kids, she was shocked to see lots of pupils there despite the outrageous school fees and how undisclosed, majority of the kids are white, half cast and billionaires dark skin kids.

All students were taught their country language and then the general language "English"

This is what I have been looking for, my kids will definitely get along here she muttered to herself. That was how Stephan and Stephanie entered Eden Nobele` High School

•••

Stephan has never been interested in all of this until recently his feelings started developing, he had known Annabel for years, so why did he start feeling this way lately.

I will like to get married to Annabel after college, he told Sammy his buddy one day, I think you should tell her how you feel bro, this issue is truly you eating you up, I also think she likes you.

Really? Why do you think so, she told you anything? Did You hear anything of such maybe from Stephanie or the other girls Stephan asked with curiosity

No, calm down bro, like I see the way you both play together, are found of each other, care for each other and kook at each other he said clearing his throat

Oh, come on, just that? we are besties what do you expect

That Friday noon, Stephan was seriously searching every was for Annabel, Where's Anny? He would ask, have you seen Annabel today? And then Ezekiel the bell ringer told him he saw Anabel heading towards the arena, he quickly ran towards the arena, as he walked in, he could hear her singing from a distance, her voice was so melodious and angelic that his heart melted, he didn't know how to approach her again, he walked gently to the middle stage where she was standing, Annabel could sense the presence of someone else, she stopped singing and turned, and there she was already a step away from Stephen, and they both stared at each other dumbfounded.

Nice song, Stephan manages to break the silence and tension between them

Hmmm... mum and I favorite song, she said looking downwards

She's not a shy type, but her emotions won't let her look straight at Stephan's eyes, look up Stephan said, Anny nodded her head negatively, I can't she said in a whisper.

You can't do what? he asked lifting her head gently with his hands

I can't do this, she burst into tears and turned to run away.

EPISODE 3
Still the One

Stephan seizes her hand, he too was confused about what to do, so he hugged her tightly, and Anny could feel his heartbeat...

Then she heard a whisper *"I Love You"*

Both were already melting inside. This sounded different from the normal best friends goodbye, I love you to Annabel

•••

I think I am in love with you Annabel, and then he knelt saying *will you marry me?*

I mean not now though Like after college he added

Anny's mouth was wide open as tears gushed out her eyes, she realized she was in love, this was her first Love.

Why are you kneeling as if you are proposing without a ring on, after college is still a long time she said laughing and blushing as she pulled him to get up...

They took a seat at the arena and started talking.

Being at the edge of leadership, I have found myself handling many matters in relationships, Said, Annabel

I sometimes ask a few students why they are into relationships, and I hear a lot of hilarious but no tangible reasons.

Some say it makes them grow up, and mature and so many reasons

Personally, when I think of dating amongst teens and very young people like us, I picture this wild rush of emotions, making out in the parking lot, kissing which usually leads to more intense kissing with sexually charged flowing hormones, wild romance, and then sex... she paused and later on, its consequences.

I see this around almost every day amongst the students, and the truth is teenage romances are usually for fun, nothing serious, they barely last long and can cause more harm than good.

Often it involves sticking, clinging, or hanging out with one person all the time, pairing you off, and isolating you from others. And if the other person gets too familiar with the opposite sex, it will spring out Jealousy, and then, of course, you will always be talked about, and then You will be the subject of discussion, assumptions, and the center of dramas, your reputation is on the line too and then one can get so carried away if not careful and fall out of grade, and finally, you two properly would get bored of each other over time quickly because of no commitment and purpose for the relationship.

And I, I don't want to be in that circle. Annabel said to Stephan

Many young persons have little or no understanding of

relationships, said Stephan

Understanding gives an edge on how to handle emotions and then spiritual maturity is also vital when it comes to relationships. So, while some let their emotions get a better place, others lack standards, ethics, and morals

The truth is that having a relationship with God first helps you have an idea of what a true relationship entails, we live in a culture that idolizes romance. If you don't have the first relationship with God, one's affection can exceed their affection for Christ. Paving the way for idolatry. Most students yield to peer pressure and are so immature and inexperienced.

And have hindered some in fulfilling God's purposes and mission of sharing the Gospel when engaging in sexual immorality.

Relationships are hugely dependent on the maturity level of the people involved.

Love is to be willing to sacrifice (your time/effort/resource) for another with no thought of a return.

So true, said Anabel, Ignorance in relationships, especially amongst young teenagers has not helped at all.

Remember how Miriam in SS2 wanted sex badly and start playing adult life early, in her ignorance, she became pregnant, and had to stop school, many who are pressured into the dating gang failed to use protective measures, leading to sexually transmitted diseases, and pregnancies that lead to abortions, abortion rate are so high, I know these because sometimes I handle some few cases with the school authorities. And I hear some from the girls.

While some others are weighed down by a partner in making valuable decisions in their life, some are dating out of pity which is disastrous, like you know it's not heading anywhere so what are you doing in there? low or high esteem the fact is that Sex makes babies, and scripture commends we flee fornication...

Japa, Stephan said *laughing...*

I also have a lot of guys complaining of clingy girls who can be frustrating.

They sort for care and attention with too much, with lots of drama, and how some beg for sex, giving out their bodies just for satisfaction and pleasure for a while...

I would rather watch the drama from the outside than be a part of it. Remember, ***marriage is honorable with the bed undefiled.***

How come you know so much about relationships asked Stephen

My mum thought me, especially from a biblical standpoint replied Annabel

When I became the senior perfect girl, she got me a sex educator and a relationship coach for lectures during the holidays, she said I was like a mother to all girls and this is the most popular practical subject I will see in school environs, and she's so right, I see them every day. often, I counsel the girls about teenage relationships... I educate as much as I can that brings their relationships and lives to me

I will enlighten my guys too, Stephan said

Building intimacy without commitment is dangerous. As teens there are little or no chances of even dating your life partner, young ones should not waste time on short-term immature relationships, at least they should all know about what they are signing in for, like read books, learn about relationships first, learn from an adult who made mistakes.

This will reduce the rate of sexual immorality and its consequences, abortions, unwanted pregnancy, sexually transmitted diseases, etc...

•••

Annabel, you are the lady of my dream, I would love to spend my life with you, but right now I want us to be focused on our future and become the very best we can, I will never mention this again until the time is ripe, God help us, if this is his will, we will be together.

I have always admired your sense of maturity you know, and sometimes I wonder where you got a balanced nature of life from, I guess is from Grandma. Said, Annabel

It's beautiful how we both have common reverence for God first, I will tell my parents about the new us, me either replied Annabel as they concluded their discussion, Annabel, and Stephan had agreed they would zip up, till the right time, and if God's will to get married it would be done...

They have been so much taught about the dangers of premarital sex; they both want to please God and be an example to others so they stayed as best friends...

EPISODE 4
Still the One

And then it was their graduation ceremony, Stephanie, Stephan, and Annabel were always among the stars in the class in their yearly magazine

They were all announced the best students in a different subject, Stephan was the best in mathematics and economics, Stephanie in two act subjects and Annabel in six science courses...

As her mother helped her pick some of her awards, they announced

Let's make welcome the overall best graduating student "Annabel Michael".

As balloons and ribbons were ripped down inside the auditorium, everyone stood up cheering and clapping and celebrating her, the soft music "stand up, stand up for the champion" started playing in the background, it was a beautiful experience.

That's my wife, Stephan muttered to himself, as he ran to Hug, congratulate and take pictures with Annabel.

As Annabel read her valedictory speech, she spoke with so much boldness and authority; she ended with this keynote

"The power within"

Let no man despise you "you have the power to allow men to

despise you and you have the power to stop them"

I Annabel Michael plead with you my fellow grandaunt, as you go out there, don't let anyone despise you. But be a model in all you do.

To all students of Eden high school, I want you to know that not dating in high school Is normal, and fine please, sexually purity is still the best, Sex is sweet but reserved for marriage alone, allow no one to fool or mount unnecessary pressure on you, be focused, be disciplined, above all love and fear God

Flee youthful lust, Abstinence is still the best.

She got a standing ovation with loud cheering, clapping, and shouting

She was indeed a model, and she will be thoroughly missed, her little impact won't be forgotten in a hurry

Senior Annabel can we take pictures with you, some came crying, kissing, and hugging.

The occasion was finally over as Annabel ran to hug her friends and parents, Congratulations everyone was saying.

•••

Months later

They went to college in different countries, yet she still connected with the twin through FaceTime.

They would gist about everything, pray together, etc.

At some point, because of multiple academic workloads, they barely talk for days and then years went by and then the time was ripe

EPISODE 5
Still The One

During courtship, the temptation between them increased, as they burn in passion for one another, But the scripture kept them "Marriage is sweet, with the bed undefiled"

I Stephan Steve take Annabel Michael as my lawful wedded wife

Sammy and Stephanie were the groom's men and the bride's maids.

And then Annabel took to sing this song by Shania Twain, her voice was more angelic than ever...

Looks like we made it

Look how far we've come, my baby

We might take the long way

We knew we'd get there someday

They said, "I bet they'll never make it"

But just look at us holding on

We're still together, still going strong

(You're still the one)

(Then Stephen joined in)

You're still the one I run to

The one that I belong to

You're still the one I want for life

(You're still the one)

You're still the one that I love

The only one I dream of

You're still the one I kiss goodnight

(Stephan took the next stanza)

Ain't nothin' better

We beat the odds together

I'm glad we didn't listen

Look at what we would be missin'

They said, "I bet they'll never make it"

But just look at us holding on

We're still together, still going strong

(Annabel joined in the Duet) and she rested her head on his chest as they were dancing ballet

You're still the one I run to

The one that I belong to

You're still the one I want for life

(You're still the one)

You're still the one that I love

The only one I dream of

You're still the one I kiss goodnight

You're still the one

The duet intensified the Love in the air, I bet you will wish to marry, for some marry again

And then they kissed each other**

Stephan and Annabel later had two kids, established lots of kingdom projects together, and lived happily ever after.

Extract from Hebrew 13:4 (NKJV)

Marriage is honorable in all, and the bed undefiled: but fornicators and adulterers God will judge.

ABOUT EPISTLE

Realities of life with kingdom solutions

Epistle can be categorized into 3 M's (Ministry, Message, Me)

1. **Epistle as a Ministry (The rise of a Generation)**

Epistle- the rise of a generation is a ministry aimed at raising young people to **Know** God, **Grow** in the knowledge of God and **Influence** their world positively for God. It is a movement to rise and raise young armies/representatives for God.

2. **Epistle as a Message (Books)**

Epistle is a letter written/spoken to the church/believers/the body of Christ concerning the things which be, and addressing issues amongst the body (the church) as becoming saint, as seen from Apostle Paul. The original founder of Epistles (Peace be unto you Sir) a laborer and prisoner of our Lord Jesus Christ

These epistles by Precious James are basically Realities of life (things happening in our daily life) with kingdom solutions. They come in short stories, and speeches, but are edifying with principles of the kingdom

3. **Epistle as Me (A person)**

I am an Epistle KNOWN and READ by all men; YOU are an Epistle- the message, the letter that we read (2 Cor. 3:2)

An epistle is an example (Pattern/Model/Template) of the believers (1 Timothy 4:12b)

Be An Epistle Today!!!

CHECK OUT OTHER LIFE-CHANGING EPISTLES BY PRECIOUS JAMES!!!

- **THE THINGS AROUND OUR NECK**
- **SECOND CHANCE**
- **COME BACK DEMAS**
- **WASTED YEARS OF YESTER-YEARS**
- **WHAT LIFE STOLE FROM ME**
- **TEARS OF WISDOM**
- **BEAUTIES OF SINGLE-HOOD**
- **UNFAIR ADVANTAGE**
- **FATHERS OF THE-MORROW**
- **THE PURSUIT OF YOUR STAR**
- **HELP US!!! THE MINISTRY OF THE AQUILIA'S**
- **NO EXCUSE**
- **WHAT NEXT? NOW THAT I AM SAVED**
- **MY HEART BEATS FOR YOU**

- **MY SEXUAL ADDICTION**
  AND LOTS MORE…

OTHER BOOKS BY THE SAME AUTHOR

Becoming books are entrepreneurship books by Precious James aimed to help you BECOME a person of value to yourself and then to the society at large, it fights laziness and gives you the positive push to start something and BECOME the best version of yourself.

1. **Bake the cake - A step-by-step guide/approach – Vol 1**
2. **Cake Decorating – Buttercream techniques - Vol 2**
3. **Advance cake decorating with fondant - Vol 3**
4. **Whipped Cream Decorating – Stable whipped cream recipe - Vol 4**
5. **How to make yummy Meat-pie – Vol 5**
6. **How to make small chops (samosa, spring roll, Puff-puff, peppered meat/chicken) – Vol 6**
7. **How to make Yummy Chin-Chin – Vol 7**
8. **How to make homemade shawarma – Vol 8**
9. **How to make Peanut Burger – EASY STEPS – Vol 9**
10. **How to make Sausage Roll – Vol 10**
11. **How to make Eggroll and Buns – Vol 11**
12. **How to make Yummy Bread – Vol 12**
13. **How to make yummy Doughnut (Ring and Pillow Doughnuts) – Vol 13**

and lots more

FOR CONTACT INFORMATION

YouTube: Epistle- The rise of a Generation

Facebook: Epistle

Instagram: Epistle worldwide

Call/WhatsApp: +2348108826904

ABOUT THE AUTHOR

PRECIOUS JAMES is a passionate lover of God, a graduate of mechanical engineering from the University of Port-Harcourt, Nigeria.

She is a Writer, Teacher of God's word, and Entrepreneur, she has her Cake and Perfume line and she is the founder of the ministry "Epistle-The rise of a Generation" she is passionate about raising a God-driving, influential, and mighty Generation

She writes Epistles, these are true life realities with kingdom solutions, divinely inspired by the holy spirit of God, so we can be an Epistle (Model, Pattern, Template) of the believers (1 Timothy 4:12b)

Connect with her on Facebook: precious James and Instagram: _preciousjames_

www.ingramcontent.com/pod-product-compliance
Lightning Source LLC
LaVergne TN
LVHW020544160826
845677LV00015B/4186

* 9 7 9 8 8 4 6 2 2 1 8 0 2 *